For Judy, Jill and all the phantom pets at No. 46

A TEMPLAR BOOK

First published in the UK in hardback in 2006 by Templar Publishing.
This softback edition first published in the UK in 2006 by Templar Publishing,
an imprint of The Templar Company plc,
Pippbrook Mill, London Road, Dorking, Surrey, RH4 1JE, UK
www.templarco.co.uk

First softback edition

ISBN-13: 978-1-84011-662-5
ISBN-10: 1-84011-662-5

Edited by Stella Gurney

Printed in China

the Elephantom

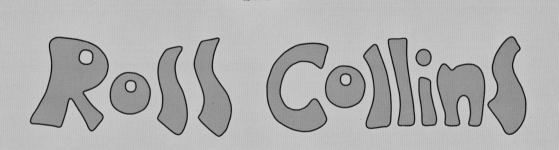

Ross Collins

templar publishing

We have an Elephantom.

He turned up on a Tuesday,
just after tea-time.

To be honest, he's starting to bug me.

He keeps me awake at night...

On Fridays he gets his friends over for parties.

I can't say it's the highlight of MY week...

Parents don't seem to notice
phantom elephants.

Dad hasn't even realised that it's
my room that always smells of dung.

"New perfume, darling? What an.

nteresting aroma."

And whenever I try to tell Mum,
she just humours me.

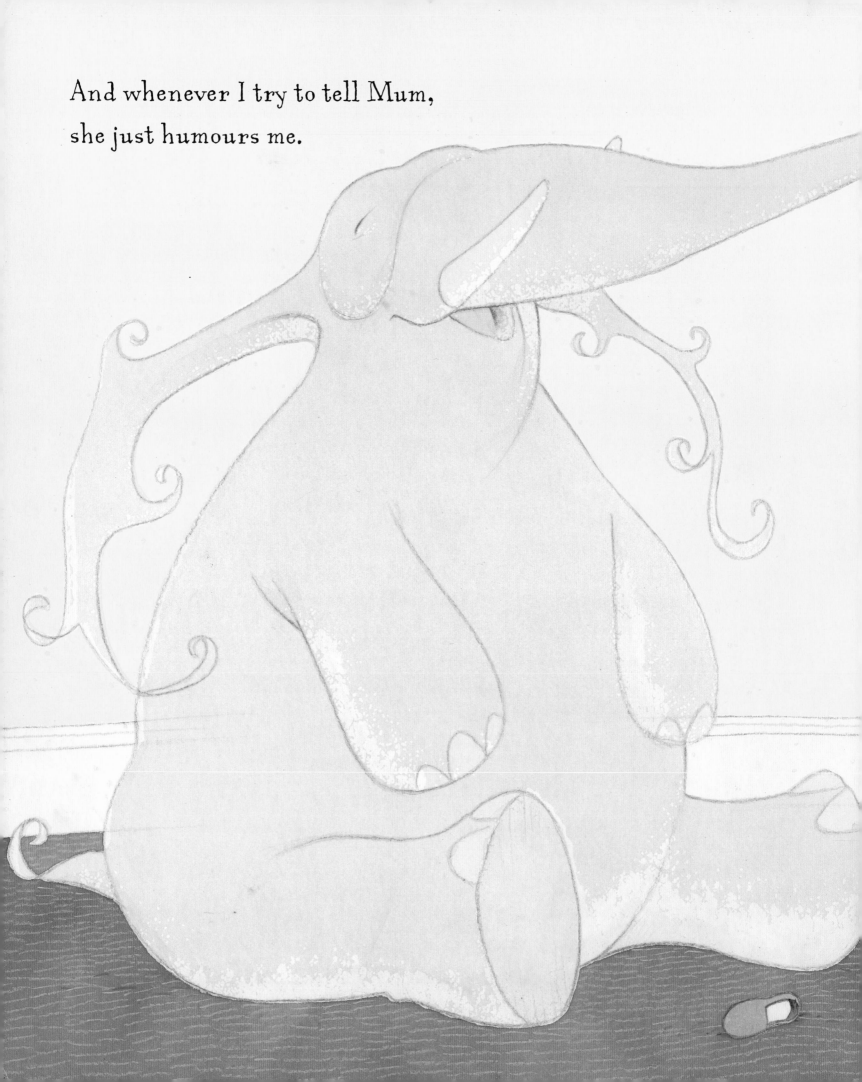

"That's nice, dear — why don't you go and tell your grandma?"

"Gran - we have an Elephantom."

"How MARvellous for you!"

I knew Gran would believe me – she has lots of ghost pets.

But when I explained that the Elephantom
was a bit of a handful and I didn't
want him any more,

Gran knew just what to do.

Spectral & Son

PURVEYORS of ODDITIES

664 Collywobble Court

CALLERS WELCOME

She rummaged around and
found an old card.

It smelled of parsnips.

"Mr Spectral will sort you out,"
she smiled.

It took me four hours and thirty-seven minutes
to find his shop.

Inside, it was dark and musty
and smelled of parsnips.
Mr Spectral's stock was... unusual.

"I want to get rid of an Elephantom,"
I said.

Mr Spectral nodded.

"I have fifty pence,"
I said.

Mr Spectral
smiled...

and gave me
a box.

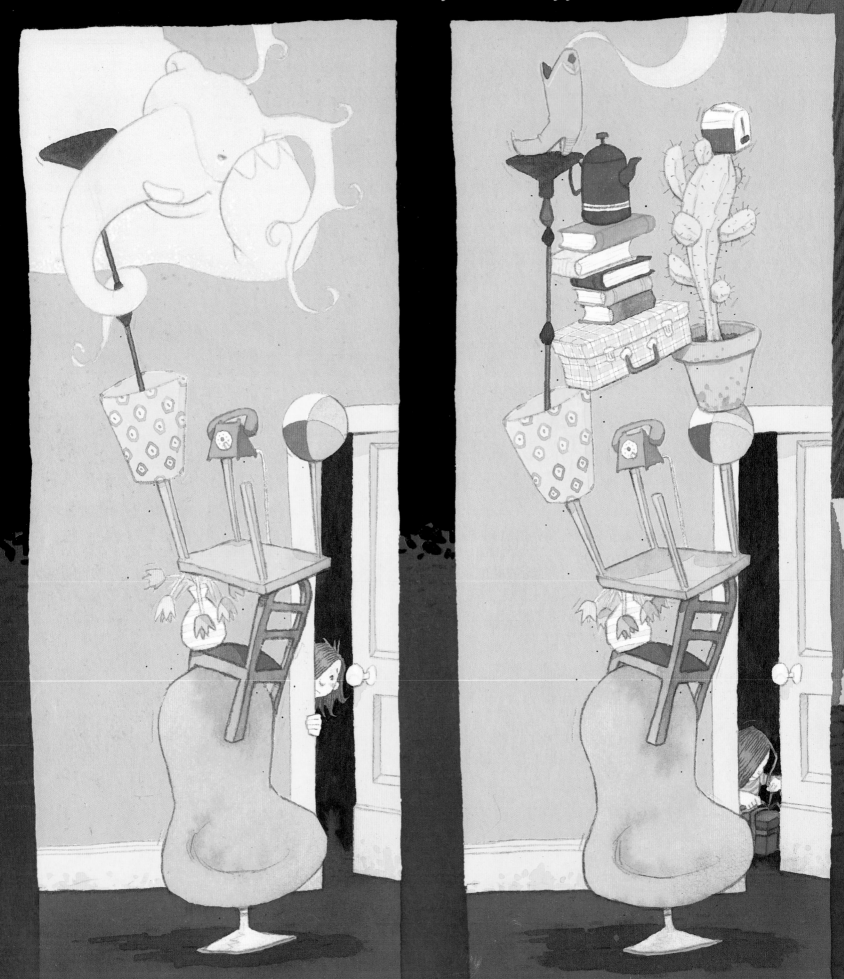

We don't have an Elephantom any more...

...but our neighbours do.